MW01247043

The Leak

A novella by
Shingi Mavima

First published in Great Britain in 2024 by:

Carnelian Heart Publishing Ltd
Suite A
82 James Carter Road
Mildenhall
Suffolk
IP28 7DE
UK
www.carnelianheartpublishing.co.uk

Copyright ©Shingi Mavima 2024

Paperback ISBN   978-1-914287-61-9

eBook ISBN   978-1-914287-62-6

This novella is entirely a work of fiction. The names, characters and incidents portrayed in it are the work of the author's imagination. Any resemblance to actual persons, living or dead, is purely coincidental.

All rights reserved. No part of this publication may be reproduced, stored in a retrieval system or transmitted in any form or by any means, electronic, mechanical, photocopying, recording or otherwise without prior written permission from the publisher.

Editors:
Memory Chirere &
Samantha Rumbidzai Vazhure

Cover design:
Artwork – Rukodzi Art
Layout – Rebeca Covers

Typeset by Carnelian Heart Publishing Ltd
Layout and formatting by DanTs Media

Table of Contents

Chapter 1   11

Chapter 2   14

Chapter 3   23

Chapter 5   30

Chapter 6   36

Chapter 7   41

Chapter 9   56

Chapter 10   61

Chapter 11   64

Chapter 12   69

Chapter 16   90

Chapter 17   93

Chapter 19   101

Glossary   116

About the author   119

Dedicated to the memory of Sekuru Gabriel Chakanetsa Gwatirisa. I just know you would have enjoyed this one.

"Isu tauya pano, dai tauya tese
Dai tiri vazhinji, nhasi taionana…"

My sincerest and unparalleled gratitude is reserved for my mother, the good Dr. Pauline Gwatirisa, whose constant support and editing far supersede what is asked of "another set of eyes" on my work, often rising to the level of quasi co-author. Thank you Maphosa. Special thanks go to my sister Michelle Mavima Morris, mainini Ruvimbo Maramwidze, Dr. Ally Day, Mazvita Zunidza, Meyling Ruiz, and Godwin Jabangwe, without whose feedback this story would have been forever confined to the doldrums of could-have-beens. I would also like to thank the remarkable Dr. Kathryn Mara, who has been a much-appreciated source of encouragement during this process.

I am forever grateful to the beautiful people at Carnelian Heart Publishing for taking a chance on this labor of pain.

Finally, to all those who continue to chase a seemingly elusive peace in their lives, this story is our story. May the hope of a more content tomorrow keep us through the night.

Chapter 1

It had been right here the last time I saw it, Kuda muttered to himself. He immediately realised the emptiness of this epiphany. He was nowhere closer to finding it than he had been half an hour ago when he had frantically excused himself from the gathering in the living room. He checked his backpack again, before dejectedly dragging his feet to the tattered suitcase. He was certain that it wasn't there. He virtually lived out of that old bag and could recite its contents at any moment with sad precision.

He had not felt his eyes well up until he saw the salted drops fall onto the backpack, to which he had unwittingly returned and was now rummaging through. Marginal hope returned as he felt a hard, book-sized object in a previously unchecked pocket. As it turned out, it was a book; his faithful notepad, dubbed *bhuku ramangwanda* some fifteen years ago. An equally tattered photograph fell onto the floor, and Kuda made haste to pick it up.

The nostalgia that finding the old book and photograph had brought lasted for two seconds, before the vexation of the present moment resurfaced. He grabbed the now-empty backpack and hurled it in blind fury across the room, collapsing onto the tiny bed upon which he had been searching for the gift. His head already in his sweaty palms, he did not see the bag almost hit Maria, now standing in the doorway of the bedroom.

Maria stood there just long enough for him to lift his head and catch the bewildered look on her face, before she turned and headed back to where the rest of the family was readying to cut the cake. He followed her begrudgingly; intent on making sure that she did not tell the festive gathering of the manic episode she had walked in on. At the very least, he wanted to be there if she decided to do so. She did not. This did little to diffuse the tension of the moment. If anything the silence, albeit lasting just a few seconds, added to the awkward air under which the room was now drowning. Thank God for Maiguru Mai Tawanda, the default matriarch of the family with Gogo refusing to move to the city, who seemed to cherish the unenviable, if futile, task of leading the pretence that everything was okay.

"Ah, Uncle Kuda, we were just waiting for you before cutting the cake...:"

"Sorry Maiguru, I was looking for..."

Kuda did not get to finish his monotonous explanation, as the festive crowd broke into a spirited rendition of 'Happy Birthday,' inspired in part by desire, nay, need to drown his odd behaviour from the rare moment of levity for which they had managed to gather in what had been a miserable season.

He felt...relieved. The relief one feels when the police car that has been tailing them for the past mile turns onto an adjacent street. He sank into an empty chair in a bid to make his gigantic frame inconspicuous to the rest of the party. This was just as well. Amidst all the anxiety and frustration, he had not realised how exhausted he was. He had just closed his eyes, partly in pursuit of elusive sleep and partly to fight back the tears that still tethered on the edges of his eyelids, when Maria drifted from the madding crowd onto the chair next to where he was.

"*Kwakanaka here?* What's going on?" she asked of her childhood friend, many moons removed from their acquaintance.

A resentful smile crept across his face. He wanted to tell her.

Chapter 2

O, how he wanted to tell her.

He wanted to tell her how he had been the last one to know that Maria and her husband, his cousin Tawanda, would be home for Christmas for the first time in over a decade. How he had only found out three days before their arrival. That two days after they arrived, at their behest, would be a birthday party for their cousin Ruramisai's daughter, Mandi. How it would be the first time he would be seeing Ruramisai and Mandi in over a year, despite living in the same sprawling city. He had scrounged through his non-existent funds to get her a gift, a sketch artist's rendition of him and his niece, based on a photo of the two of them that he kept in his wallet. Sure, it was sentimental drivel whose weight may have been lost on the six-year-old, but this was hardly about her. Since before she was born, she had heard tales of her American uncle and every holiday and birthday until now had been punctuated with toys and books from overseas. And now, the said American uncle was here—toys, books, wife and all. He had something Uncle Tawanda did not have though: he had been there, and this picture would be proof of that. Maybe not to Mandi, but the adults would know. Maria and Tawanda would know.

He wanted to remind her how good friends they had been during the early years of high school. His mother had died when he was six. The Creature got her. Because she had moved to the city while he had stayed behind in Watsomba with Gogo, nothing much had changed for the boy after she passed—aside from Mhai's seasonal visits and the little money she would send for his upkeep. If anything, he distinguished himself by being dominant in his studies: the gap between him and the rest of his classmates made a mockery of the idea of cohort parity. Thus, when he turned twelve and on the cusp of high school, and with fears of Gogo's waning health, his aunt and uncle, Mai and Baba Tawanda, decided to take him in. It would do him well to spend some time in the big city. Besides, they had taken in another of their nieces, Ruramisai, a few years earlier: the three cousins would be a healthy support system for each other. By then, Tawanda was already in high school at arguably the best boys' school in the country. Arguably; the topic never failed to come up whenever Tawanda or his father, an old boy of the same school, were around their friends from rival schools whose century-old colonial legacies put them in an enclave that may well have been hidden from the rest of the country.

One year younger than Tawanda, Kuda enrolled at the local co-ed school instead; the same one that Ruramisai, who happened to be in the same grade, attended. Once upon a simpler time, it had been one of the better schools in town. Unlike Tawanda's, school, which had been exclusively for White students until sixty years into its existence, the local co-ed had been built in 1982, a crowning jewel in the recently independent government's attempts to rectify the historical imbalances between the elites and the masses. At some point in the following decades, it appears the government had abandoned the noble cause, and this erstwhile pretence at an institution of top learning served as an enduring reminder of what might have been. Enrolling Kuda at Tawanda's arguably best boys' school in the country would not only have cost too much, but it would also have been a bridge too far for a boy transplanted from rural Watsomba. For what it mattered, the local co-ed school was a bridge too far. Initially, Kuda had found comfort from the rabid teasing of his city-bred classmates in Ruramisai's company. In time, however, the burden of carrying Kuda socially through a school she was relatively new to herself grew too cumbersome for Ruramisai, although she would never say it. Soon, she was making up excuses to sit with other people and not be where Kuda was, occasionally meeting him on the walk back home. He may not have been raised in the city, but Kuda was no fool. He knew what was happening and, as much as it stung, he understood.

On his walk home from school, Kuda would stop by Mai Lazzie's market, if for nothing else, to feel like he belonged somewhere. He did not spend what little pocket money he got on hot dogs and Cokes like his classmates and cousin did. The very idea! For the price of one of each, he could haul at least half a grocery bag of guavas, *mazhanje*, and *mauyu* from Mai Lazzie's. Not only did they taste better, but they also reminded him of Watsomba. Granted, back in Watsomba, he never had to pay; just easy pickings on the way to school and meadows. He remembered how his old friend Kurauone had climbed up a *muzhanje* tree once, only to lose his footing and fall right onto his startled dog! As he chuckled to himself, his daydream was interrupted by calls of "Wasu! Wasu!" from two boys. He didn't know their names, but he recognised them as part of the Taliban Crew, a group of Form Two boys who modelled themselves after what they called Dipset or G Unit. American rap groups, Kuda had gathered. They wore red and blue winter coats that were way too big, even for the most bitter of Zimbabwean winters. The aesthetic was especially ridiculous, as those winter coats were often accompanied by baggy basketball shorts and tan boots, seemingly designed for walking in the bush. Oh, and they spoke in affected American accents, just to drive the point home.

"Wasu! Have you been hunting and gathering?" the de facto leader of the Taliban, duly nicknamed Osama, yelled out as the group encircled Kuda like hyenas, roaring in sinister glee.

Kuda stood still. He was tired. Too tired to be scared or embarrassed. As the boys drew closer, one of them reached for the plastic bag, tearing it and sending the fruit tumbling onto the street. As weary tear trickled down his face, Kuda remained statuesque.

Disappointed by the apparent lack of reaction from their prey, Osama snuck around and pulled down Kuda's shorts, much to the rabid laughter of his gang and the other Form Two students who had gathered around since. The furore had also caught the attention of Mai Lazzie from inside the market. She came out, broom in hand, to see what the commotion was about. She may have meant to just tell the boys to keep it down but, recognizing her timid loyal customer at the centre, she charged towards the malaise, feverishly swinging her broom.

"*Musiyei!* Leave that poor child alone!"

The Taliban crew stood back, arrogant in their caution. They were certain she would not hit them that close to the school—she would never be able to work in the market again.

"You!" she screamed, gesturing at Osama, "Are you not Enoch, Mai
Muradzikwa's boy?"

He was.

"When did you become this way? Is it this American fuck music that has changed you?"

Osama smirked, and his friends dropped their heads as their smiles faded.

"I remember you. I used to clean your house, remember me? Just two years ago I was hanging up your blankets after you wet them each night, and now you feel like a big boy because you wear that oversized jacket and are in high school. *Tibvire apa mhani*!"

The laughter turned onto Osama, beginning with the crowd that had since gathered. Osama, now the centre of more attention than he typically received, and not for reasons he usually sought it, looked around, reaching for a response. Realising he had nothing for Mai Lazzie, he turned around to the rest of the Taliban, announcing in a heightened American accent as he stormed off, "Aayt yo, let's bounce!"

The rest of his friends, heads still down, were stifling giggles. They made as if to follow him, before breaking into fits of laughter with the rest of the crowd once Osama was a few feet away. He looked back, but the rest of the Taliban had now blended into the crowd, where someone had started the chant, "Enoch, *chinja ma*sheets! Enoch, *chinja ma*sheets!" and everyone joined in.

Kuda knew Maria remembered this part. He knew because he had not seen or heard any of this. As he cried, standing still, his head had been under the big *muzhanje* tree in Watsomba. He pulled up his shorts and gathered his baobabs and a few of the guavas—the ones that were still intact. The baobab fruit has a thick outer shell. It is good like that. It was Maria that, a few weeks later, had told him what had happened.

As he knelt to the ground, she had come over to him, bringing two baobab fruits that had strayed furthest and a plastic bag from her own backpack.

"Here, comrade, use this instead." she said, getting on her knees to gather the rest with him. He grabbed the plastic bag and, without acknowledging her otherwise, got up and began walking home.

"*Aizve* comrade!" Maria yelled as she paced after him, "that's no way to thank a lady!"

Although he did not reply, he allowed her to catch up with him.

"You are the new kid at the Mapfundes, right? Tawa and Rura's cousin."

Kuda nodded, still jaded and rather sceptical of the strange girl's intentions.

"Those are my peoples! Tawanda and I? Best of friends! Haha. Well, not so much since we finished primary school and went our separate ways. I barely see him now and, when I do, he's with a whole new clique. *Ini ah!*"

Kuda chuckled a little, coming back to earth. She caught his smile, and she smiled back, as she rubbed the back of his head familiarly, like the city people did with their dogs.

"You're alright...Kuda, is it? Don't let the Taliban get you down, you heard what Mai Lazzie said about Osama," she said, laughing out loud as she did.

He smiled again and nodded, even though he had no idea what Mai Lazzie had said. He would not know until a few weeks later, when the shame of the humiliation that had brought them together, and his timidity, had begun to wear off. She had told him the whole story for the first time; the first of many retellings during their teen years.

But on that day, she had checked her phone in panic and, as strangely as she had come to his aid, she burst into a sudden sprin —presumably home— yelling out "give my greetings to Tawa and the family!" as she did.

This was the first story he had ever written in the tattered notebook.

Maybe she remembered.

Chapter 3

"What? Oh, it's nothing. You know...this living. It's up and it's down. Some days are better than others!" Kuda responded to Maria, before Ruramisai interrupted the nascent conversation with two slices of cake, one for each of them. Kuda was in no mood for cake, but did not want to draw any more attention, negative or otherwise. Besides, the interruption and cake bought him time away from a conversation he was not particularly keen on having.

"This turned out well, no?" Maria said, turning to Ruramisai, perhaps also dissuaded from pursuing the conversation with Kuda.

Just as well.

Kuda stood up and, waving inconspicuously, made for the door.

No sooner had he stepped out when, to his disappointment, Tawanda yelled out as he paced towards him "Ah Kuda, were you leaving? Without saying anything? *Asi chiiko?*"

He felt guilty. Not for leaving the party, it was surely almost done anyway. Besides, it is not like he was the life of it. If anything, he was certain the festivities would turn up a notch without his heavy presence. He felt guilty because he knew and, as archaic as it may be, respected protocol. And protocol dictated that you did not leave without bidding everyone farewell. Especially at a family celebration. Especially not while the guests from overseas were still making merry.

"Yeah. Sorry," he responded, with far less enthusiasm than with which the question had been asked, "You know this touch-and-go life of ours. Whenever the money wakes up, you have to be ready!"

"Aah. Hustler!" Tawanda chuckled, pretending to understand Kuda, "tell you what? We leave next weekend, Maria and I. Why don't we do coffee before then? Say, tomorrow at 8 *pa...*, what's that new joint called— Beanster?"

Kuda gave a wry nod as Tawanda leaned in for a handshake and embrace, slipping his cousin a crumpled-up note.

He gave one more sombre wave, before disappearing into the early evening.

He debated catching a kombi to his apartment, then decided against it. He needed the exercise, and home was only 30 minutes away by foot. Sure, it was dark out already, but it was a brisk summer evening, and he knew these streets well. Besides, he did not have any money on him.

Money. He remembered the note Tawanda had handed him. He fumbled around for it in his pocket, and guessed it was five American dollars. It was too worn to be a much bigger bill and felt too clean to be the filthy one or two dollar bills doing their rounds here. Granted, his cousin had probably brought it with him from overseas, so who knows if any of this applied?

He was right. It was five dollars.

The nerve of him. Does he think I need his money? How does he think I have been living this whole time? Does he even know? And five dollars? If he wanted to be charitable, why not be really charitable?

Now he wants to do "coffee?" Hah! Who "does coffee" here? At 8am? Please. What does he think this is, New York City? Kuda could not recall the last time he had had coffee, even at home.

Doing coffee. I ought not to go. Tell him I am coming and not show up. Hah! No. He will run and tell everyone, Maria and all, how I am such a failure because I cannot be counted on, even to do coffee. I will go. Wear my pointed leather shoes and cashmere scarf. He will see. I am not a bum. I am not like these other boys here.

I was not meant to be, anyway. Does he know that?

By now, Kuda was climbing up the rusty metal stairs to his second-floor city studio apartment. The elevator had been dead going on five years now. Unlocking his door, he collapsed onto the queen-sized mattress on the floor. The power was out again, and he made no effort to light the candles.

He stared at the ceiling. Sometimes when it rained hard, water would drip onto the edge of his bed.

Thankfully, not tonight though. Tonight, the room was flooded with his disjointed thoughts.

Now, where was he?

Chapter 4

Since the incident at Mai Lazzie's market, Maria and Kuda had walked home together. Well, she walked him home. She figured that, for as long as she was with him, the Taliban and what was left of their pride, would be a little more hesitant to humiliate Kuda again. In exchange, she got to hear the wild, exotic stories he brought with him from Watsomba. She even tried out the fruits he bought at the market. Although Mai Lazzie and others had been there her whole life, she had never even thought about the market. She found she liked *mauyu*, once she got over the chalky texture. *Mazhanje*—not so much.

All things considered; it was a good deal for both. Maria came from a stricter family than most in the community. She never spoke about her home life, but Kuda had pieced this together from her sudden bursts towards home each time her phone rang, and the murmurs about her father, the war veteran-turned-dentist. He would drive by the school every now and then, slowly, as if inspecting the royal guard and, like the royal guard, those who knew him would stand statuesque on the side of the road until he passed.

Naturally, then, the boys knew to stay away from her. Kuda, however, was disarming. Besides being the rural anomaly at the school, he was two years her junior. It also did not hurt his budding ego that, by many a whisper among the boys, Maria was among the prettiest girls in school. If, for no other reason, she was not the worst company to be seen with. In earnest, however, he was just glad to have some semblance of a friend, even as their fellowship mostly constituted uneventful walks home together after school.

Until the holiday party.

Through his friendship with Maria, Kuda had pieced together that his uncle, Baba Tawanda, and Maria's mother had been college friends-turned-business partners in the 1980s up until the late 1990s. Exporting things. Or was it importing? Kuda did not quite get what his uncle did, except that he travelled across Africa all the time. With the partnership spanning their single college years until both got married and began raising families, Baba Tawanda and Mai Maria's family had spent a lot of time together when the children were younger. Once, Maria recalled with a wistful glare, the two families vacationed together for two weeks, travelling across Zimbabwe and into South Africa. Then three years before Kuda moved to the city, Maria continued as the glee fled from her voice, the friendship between the two families stopped. Seemingly overnight, the business broke up and, despite continuing to leave mere minutes from each other, there were no more parties or vacations—cross border or otherwise. The apparent rift coincided with Maria starting high school, so she had not been able to follow up with Tawanda to see if he knew what was going on. In any case, he was none the wiser.

The invite to the holiday party, then, had been somewhat of a surprise. Indeed, three years had passed, but they had also passed without much interaction between the two families. At least as far as Maria and, later, Kuda were concerned. Their friendship seemed to exist in a vacuum of what used to be community.

Chapter 5

Kuda checked the time on his phone again. He had been lying down for hours, it seemed. Just as well, he hoped. He had to be in the city for some job he had been invited to for the day at 6am. He figured that, if indeed it was almost morning as he imagined, he would avoid the battle of having to wake up early by not sleeping at all. In any case, he had found sleep especially evasive in recent times. The leak in the roof, he told himself. The damned leak. In parts of his reckoning rarely visited these days, he knew his frustrations were not borne of a mere leak. He was making a decision, conscious or otherwise, not to dwell on it. He could not afford it.

It was only 11pm. He groaned. The electricity was still out.

His mind wandered across the room and, finding nothing worth focusing on, trudged back to the Christmas party a decade ago.

It may have been the presence of other families, or that the children spent much of the time playing by the pool and away from the adults, but Kuda could barely make out any semblance of disagreeability among the guests. The stereo blared out an eclectic selection, from Deep Purple to Yvonne Chaka Chaka to Simon Chimbetu. The men stood over the barbecue grill, feigning interest and knowledge of whatever topic was brought up. The women held court indoors, occasionally beckoning one of the children to deliver a message to the grill.

A few hours into the festivities, as Leonard Zhakata's *Mugove* readied to switch from pensive brooding to dancehall anthem, Maria's father signalled for the volume to be turned down. Amidst the jovial groans of protest, he struck his glass with a fork and called for the party's attention. Although he had had a drink or two, he retained the regal poise that made him equal parts intimidating and admirable. He glanced in the direction of his wife and, as if on cue, she strutted over and buried herself under his raised arm.

"Thank you, thank you..." He cleared his throat and beckoned the guests to gather around him.

"Thank you so much for celebrating with us tonight. The family and I appreciate it. Not only because we get to see you beautiful people, which is always a delight," he began, amidst awkward chuckling from the guests, "but, as is no secret to anyone here, things have been hard and are not getting easier in this country. As God would have it, our forty years in the jungle..."

"It's the wilderness, honey," his wife interjected, her hand futilely covering her mouth to both stifle giggles and confine her comment to a whisper. Everyone would have laughed too, if they were not rapt in anticipation.

"Are you sure? Okay then. The resident chaplain has corrected me. Our forty years in the wilderness are coming to an end. Only in this case, we are not headed to Egypt, but to the United States. Thank you for coming to break bread with us before we leave," he declared with an aplomb, that on any other day, would have been punctuated with cheers from the crowd.

But not today. The applause was timid, barely covering the confused murmurs that garnished the air. The party had been surprise enough; but why gather already-estranged friends and acquaintances just to announce you were leaving for good?

Seemingly oblivious to the stir, Maria's father concluded his remarks with "the night is young, gentleladies! Party on!" before waltzing off into a brief dance with his wife. Everybody drifted back into their sections, still muttering indistinctly to each other, as the music came back on.

Back by the pool, everybody congratulated Maria, hugging her in premature farewell, amidst yelps of "How long have you known!?" and "do you know when you're leaving?" Ruramisai shed a tear or two, chuckling as she embraced Maria.

Kuda stood around, feigning the same levity as his peers. After a few minutes, as the excitement died down, he strolled over to the other side of the pool, futilely attempting to remain inconspicuous as he did. He took his shoes off and dipped his feet in as he fought back tears. He prayed to be carried anywhere else but there, lest anybody saw him in this moment. The wind must have been listening, for the moment his legs touched the water, he found himself whisked back to Watsomba. He and Kurauone used to swim in the river on their way back from school, or when the cows were in the meadow. He wondered how his old friend was doing. Gogo had made somewhat of a recovery over the past few years, and the thought of her made him smile. He should go see her soon.

His momentary return to utopic Watsomba was interrupted by another pair of feet splashing the water next to him. Rapt in his ruminations, Kuda had not seen that his tears were now in free fall. Under the cover of dark, nobody else had seen them either, but his discreet departure had not gone unnoticed by Maria. She crept up, sat next to him and gazed towards the same stars as he was, her feet also in the water.

"I had no idea until last week," she finally said, her voice cracking after half a minute staring into space.

"You should have told me right away," he responded with an assertiveness that bordered on anger. Maria had never seen him like this.

"What would that change? And are you even thinking about me? I had to process it too, you know…"

Kuda did not respond.

"What did you do when you left Watsomba? Did you tell Kurauone right away?"

"It is not the same… I can always go back to Watsomba! You…" he stopped, partly feeling seen because she remembered Kurauone from his stories, and partly realising he was betraying his typical stoicism.

"I'll be back too, what do you mean? And I can bet you Kura felt the same way you are feeling now…"

"Kurauone and I are not like you and me, Maria! I…"

"What, Kuda, what?'

"You are my only friend around here, that's all…"

Throughout the entire conversation, they had not looked at each other. She placed her hand gently on top of his, which had remained planted on the ground next to him. As they continued to stare into the night sky, Maria broke the silence by a way of a chant familiar to both of them:

"Enoch, *chinja masheets!* Enoch, *chinja masheets!*"

Kuda chuckled as he wiped tears, before joining into the chant, breaking into laughter as he did.

Their moment was interrupted by a huge splash. The rest of the group had decided to bid farewell to the home by throwing each other into the pool. A gasping Tawanda swam to where they sat, his clothes drenched.

"What are you two lovebirds talking about?" he chuckled, as he splashed water in the direction of Kuda and Maria.

"Oh, nothing!" they said simultaneously. Tawanda barely heard them though, as he scrambled to get out of the water, flooding the poolside as he did.

As it were, drenched Tawanda interrupted Kuda's recollection now, just as he had interrupted them back then.

Kuda checked his phone once more and committed himself to sleep for a few hours then.

Chapter 6

"You know, perhaps the scarf and shoes may be a bit much, no?" Kuda mused as he dragged himself up from his mattress. He had never cared to appear fashionable—not like the other young people in the city did, anyway. He was no slob, not by a long way. He took great pride in oiling and combing his increasingly luscious beard, and resented the apathy with which many young men and women went about city business without deodorant. But for clothes, he cared little. He kept it simple: he had a pair of jeans, one formal pair of pants, and a few plain shirts.

When his mother was still alive, she would send him clothes from the city. Even then, he had felt peculiar, as he would then stand out from among the other children in the village. In a morbid silver lining, he had been relieved when, after his mother died, the clothes stopped coming, except for the occasional present from Baba and Mai Tawanda. After he moved to the city, he subsisted mostly on hand-me-downs from Tawanda. Even then, he curated with care the least conspicuous of the lot: not only was he not given to being ostentatious, but he figured these would be less immediately recognisable as having once belonged to his older cousin. The pursuit of the inconspicuous in fashion had stayed with him as he got older.

He had made an exception, once, in his final year of high school. By then, Tawanda was in the USA as well and, with his father gone, had taken to sending his mother a few hundred dollars here and there. Not that she needed it or wanted him to; she still earned decent money. Tawanda, perhaps eager to step into his father's shoes or consumed by warped guilt at having left when he did, sent the money anyway despite her protests. Ever the consensus-finder, she decided to let him send the money as he so wished, and she would split as much of it between Ruramisai and Kuda as was possible without feeling like she was spoiling them. Just as well, Kuda thought. He, much like his aunt—albeit for different reasons, did not much care to be on the receiving end of Tawanda's generosity. On the other hand, money is money; especially when it is the mighty American dollar. Kuda compromised with himself. He would only use the money for kombis and other necessities, and would only treat himself if he was able to make some profit on the rest. If negotiating between the time spent in rural Watsomba and suburban Harare had made anything of the boy, he had learnt to slither into spaces, unnoticed and eventually unfazed. His perennial unassuming air disarmed even battle-hardened warriors. This time, the battle-hardened warriors he came up against were the downtown Harare moneychangers. Notoriously tribal (if their tribe was other established moneychangers), they opened up to Kuda in ways not typical to the trade. It did not hurt his cause, of course, that he initially came bearing American money. Soon, he had ingratiated to the warriors and spent the rest of his Easter holidays in their midst, buying and selling currencies like Mai Lazzie sold baobab fruits. By the end of the break, he had mastered the trade and garnered himself a tidy surplus. If he did this the next holiday and, depending on what lay beneath finishing high school, perhaps a bit into the following year, he would be able to move out of Mai Tawanda's house. Maybe get an apartment in town. Who knows, maybe even enrol for a course or two.

Before then, however, stood the small matter of the leaver's dance that coming term. Kuda had not intended to go. While he had eventually worked his way into some circles at the high school after a troubled first two years, he still much preferred his own company. He did not imagine he would keep in touch with anyone from the school after they were done. Attending the dance would be nice though. He would not bring a date. Too much work. But he had promised himself a treat earlier. After putting away the money he intended to use to move out, and sending half of the rest to Watsomba, he went shopping for clothes. He had wanted to go uptown, make a trip of it. In the end, he decided to spend his money in the same downtown streets from whence his riches had come. He knew these parts and could even haggle as needs be. So he did. Marching to a small boutique-styled booth in the Indian part of downtown whose owner he had sold British pounds to, he began rummaging through the apparent high-class brands on show. He had heard they were fake. He would not have recognised the names anyway. He just wanted something that looked good. The first thing that caught his eye was a pair of glistening black dress shoes with pointed tips and a cracked design meant to approximate crocodile skin. The surface shone so bright that Kuda could see himself. He chuckled. Setting the shoes aside, he found a beige velvet blazer and beige tie to match and threw in a black dress shirt into the ensemble. Now he was ready to go. He haggled as was custom, but feeling rich and generous did not press the merchant too much. In appreciation, the merchant had thrown in a black and grey woollen scarf, with loose threads at either end that had been made either by Hollywood crazies or a Gogo somewhere who had knit it based on the description of a scarf but without ever seeing one. Haha! Kuda liked it. It looked like the sort of thing that nobody else at the dance would have. At the very least, it was the sort of thing nobody would expect him to wear.

He had outgrown the blazer and shirt since then. For the life of him, he could not remember where the tie was. But on occasion, and oh what rare occasion it had since become, he would bring out the old woollen scarf and shiny black shoes.

He washed his face and armpits under the cold running water in the sink. It was only 6am, but the fear of oversleeping had kept him on edge all night. Besides, he rather enjoyed the early morning walk around the neighbourhood and into town. The misty dawn wind brushing his face was one of the last remaining vestiges of Edenic rural life that he could still find, while the hustle and bustle at daybreak made him feel like he was part of the machine that was the big city—even when the day did not amount to much else.

The scarf and shoes it was going to be. In any case, Tawanda left before he got them, and had not been back since. Besides, who knows what may come up after doing coffee. Worst case scenario, nothing would happen, and he would just come back home and hang up his outfit for another day.

Chapter 7

Because he had wanted to walk the streets as day broke, Kuda arrived at Beanster a full hour before the shop opened. He should have thought of that, he told himself, before shrugging. How would he have known what happened in these parts of town? Sure, he walked by here once or twice a week, but he existed in a realm parallel to the green-grass people and returning diasporans who shopped and broke bread there. He stood by the coffee shop doors for a few moments, until he saw a security guard coming his way.

Trouble, he thought to himself. These guys are not used to seeing his kind in these establishments. He could never figure out if it was a directive from the phantom bosses or their desperate clinging to what little status the proximity to wealth their job gave them, but he found security guards in these areas obnoxious and aggressive.

He was thus surprised when the guard spoke to him.

"Sorry sir, but the coffee shop doesn't open for another hour or so."

"*Eish! Haa* thank you *mudhara*. No problem, I'll just…" he retorted coyly, having recovered from temporary paralysis, before noticing that the guard had already turned his back and was talking to someone else.

Sir, huh! That was unusually nice of him, Kuda thought. He could not remember the last time anyone had called him sir—if ever. He then remembered his scarf and shoes, and smiled wryly. He wanted to rally against the superficiality of the 'respect' he had just received. Such materialistic phonery. Such symbolic decadence! Where was the *ubuntu* in all this?

Despite still consciously crafting this dissenting opinion, he noticed a smile creeping across his face. He resisted for a bit before giving up. It felt...nice to be seen. Sir. Him? Besides, is that not why he had worn the scarf and shoes? Who was he to starve himself out of the simple pleasures that others—men weaker, dumber, or more unscrupulous than him— received free of charge daily? Perhaps not entirely free of charge but, you know.

As Kuda negotiated principle with himself, he had unwittingly strolled over to the other side of the shopping centre, where a teenage boy leaned by the wall, passively selling the day's newspaper.

"*The Herald* for you, *big man*?"

There it was again. Kuda made as if to search for coins in his pocket, although he had no intention of buying the paper.

"*Eish mfanami*, I don't think I have anything on me," he said, reaching down to grab a copy of the paper anyway as he did. The boy looked at him in annoyed protest, but quickly resigned to letting it be. Kuda was the first potential customer he had seen in twenty minutes; a lifetime in the roadside newspaper industry. Besides, people hardly buy the paper these days. If I am nice enough, perhaps the stranger will leave me a coin or something.

"Aren't you supposed to be in school anyway?" Kuda asked as he flipped through the newspaper with all the affected casualness of somebody wearing his scarf and shoes.

"*Ah mudhara...ma* one…" the paperboy said, and Kuda immediately felt bad for asking. He buried his head deeper into the paper, muttering to himself about bad journalism and corruption. Flipping past the entertainment section, he decided to throw his young friend a bone, reading aloud a headline about two Zimdancehall artists who had been feuding. He did not care much for the genre, or music in general, but he knew enough to know that the kids especially loved it. As expected, the boy's face lit up at the mention of the icons of his day.

"*Ah big man*! The Mbare Terrorist may talk a big game, but *pafeya chaipo*, he is not even on the same level as the Ghetto Sultan!"

"*Aah mfana*, are you serious?" Kuda responded, feigning enthusiasm, spurred on by seeing the paperboy's sudden animation. Neither of the names the boy had thrown his way were the ones mentioned, so he scurried through it closer to see if he could match the nicknames with the ones in the article. The boy was too rapt in his monologue to notice that Kuda was only half-listening.

Their conversation was interrupted by the loud honking of a car, slicing through the somber serenity of early morning Harare like a butcher's knife through a paw paw. It was Tawanda.

"Yo Wasu!" Tawanda yelled out from the car, poking his head through the window. Kuda winced at the mention of his erstwhile high school nickname. Distracted, he tossed the newspaper back towards the boy and muttered his farewells without looking at him. Had Kuda looked back, he may have seen the boy crouching to reorder the pages of the paper, too jaded to be angry. But he did not, instead he greeted his cousin with an affected chuckle and embrace. He caught a glance of the security guard over his cousin's shoulder, letting him know the coffee shop was open with a grin.

"So, do you come here often?" Tawanda asked robotically, burying himself into the menu as he sat down.

Often? Kuda winced. Am I the one who even suggested this place?

"No…well, sometimes. When business calls," he responded with no inflection. Technically true. Just last year, he had walked over there and joined a construction party working on extending the shopping mall for about two weeks. It was a decent cheque, especially in the short term. Since then, he walked past every now and then to see if anything else had come up.

"It's perfect for business, isn't it?" Tawanda said, putting down the menu excitedly. "The internet here is…mwah! He said as his eyes lit up, kissing his hand as he did. Kuda smiled wryly. Their idea of business was as divergent as their persons had become.

The barista approached their table and, before she could ask, Tawanda clamoured "Hey sweetheart! What's a couple of handsome millennials gotta do to get served in this joint?" before winking at Kuda. His cousin repeated his wry smile, nodding his head, before shaking it once his cousin looked away.

"We'll have…let's see here. I'll have a bacon and egg croissant, and a grande mocha latte. For the fine gentleman here, what will you be having, *Wasu*?"

"Just a cup of tea, please," Kuda replied, not having once looked at the menu.

"*Aaah, Wasu!* Are you intermittent fasting, Keto dieting? You know I'm paying, right?" Tawanda said amidst cackles, poking the barista on the hip with his elbow as he did. Kuda and the barista locked eyes, for but a second, and offered each other an exasperated smile. She knew what Kuda was dealing with here. She saw it at least twice a week. It might even be the reason the cafe existed, she often mused.

"One tea, one large mocha, and a croissant coming right up!" she announced as she scurried away from the table, almost certainly rolling her eyes once her back was turned.

"So, what's been up man? Any chicks in your life lately?"

Kuda chuckled to himself. He had not heard that term since high school.

"Meh. Not really. For a short while last year, I had a constant supply…"

"Nice!"

"But the space and stench in my apartment, *eish*. I would have to sell them along within a few weeks to make it worth my while. So now I do eggs instead."

Tawanda stared at him in amused confusion, before finally catching on and breaking into rabid laughter!

"Hah, you bastard! That's why we used to call you *Tsuro Magen'a*, the trickster! Chicks for sale. Hahaha!"

Kuda chuckled again. Nobody had ever called him *Tsuro Magen'a*.

"What about you, man? Maria huh!"

"Yea I know, right? Did you know her back in high school?

Kuda winced. He felt invisible again, just as he had at the birthday party the previous day. Before then, he had not felt this way in years. Not since being hounded by the Taliban a decade or so ago.

"Yes, I did," he responded, almost wistfully.

"Of course, of course. You were there when we used to hang out! Well, you know they moved to the US at some point. Soon after that, Baba had begun making arrangements for us to move as well. This place was turning to...well, you don't need me to tell you that. We had everything set up in my final year; you would have been in lower six then, right? The parents were just waiting for me to finish high school before we left."

Kuda had never heard the story told, but knew what came next. For once he noticed his cousin, famed for his obnoxious ebullience, descend into sadness.

"Then, of course, Baba passed away."

They both took subdued, ceremonial sips of their drinks, which the barista had dropped off quietly during their conversation.

"Mom decided then that she did not want to move without Baba. But, since my plans for college were already in place, we decided I should leave anyway. Maria's family would be there to receive me and help me settle…"

"See, and that surprised me," Kuda responded with the rigidity of a television interviewer, "because, I thought there had been some tension between the two…"

"Ah so you heard about that? Hah, these old people. I never knew what that was all about either. But according to *mhamha*, they had started to mend the fence, build the bridge, whatever, when Baba died. So, I guess team Maria felt like they owed us one, haha!"

He took a heavy breath, before finishing with relieved aplomb.

"Well, one thing led to another and, boom, the big guy put a ring on it haha!"

"Just like that?"

For a moment, Tawanda's cartoonish glee waned. He gazed into space, almost looking...sad.

"Yeah man, just like that," he started again, desperately attempting to capture his prior ebullience, "you know how the big dog do! Awooo! Awooo!" He howled, amidst laughter, much to the annoyance of nearby patrons.

Kuda chuckled.

"So where do you live now, boss?" Tawanda asked, eager to change the conversation.

"Haa, right in town..." It was Kuda's turn to be apprehensive. He just hoped he would not ask.

"Let's go see it man." But he did ask.

"Maybe some other time *mudhara*. I'm meeting with a client shortly, and I have to get going soon."

"Aaah Wasu. You should have told this client to meet us here. Your tea is not even cold yet!"

"I know, *mudhara*. Tight. But this is the city and its people..." Kuda retorted, reaching for his pocket. Tawanda lightly slapped his hand in protest, shaking his head as he did.

"The city indeed. Well okay. But listen. *Mhomz* spoke to us, the wife and me. And I agreed with her. She asked if I...well, she feels that your life is not going anywhere."

"Oh yea?" Kuda winced, signature slight wry smile creeping across with resentful caution. "So, what did you all decide to do with my life?"

Tawanda was taken aback, perhaps for the first time, by Kuda's seeming agitation. He had never seen him like this. Or had he? No, never. Wasu was an unbothered class act! Well, class act may be taking it too far. He was still Wasu. But unbothered nevertheless! That's why he liked him.

"*Hezvo*, Kuda! What's with the attitude? We were just tryi…"

"No pressure, comrade. What did you all think I should do?"

Tawanda hesitated, vexed further by his cousin's sudden return to his usual lethargic nonchalance.

"Well, you know, my startup is looking for new talent. You know a bit about computers, don't you?"

More than you, Kuda wanted to say. He had built half a dozen websites for local small businesses. The money had been negligible, but the work had been rewarding in other ways. He had also taught himself to dismantle and reassemble computers from seeming scraps; first by watching videos, but he could do it from memory now, he was sure. Anyway, why was he…

"Yea, I know a bit."

"But of course. Hustler! Haha. Well, if you would be interested, we are working on our internship program. It's not much to start off. But it at least gets you out of this shithole, as our president would say, hehe! People like you, that's who we need. People who know to keep their heads down, shoulder to the plough types—you know all about that, don't you, Wasu, *eh*?"

"This is all too gracious of you," Kuda mumbled, by now frantically tapping his foot under the table.

"Well, let me know! Much like our breakfast here, the offer is on the table! Ha ha ha!But…back to the chickens and eggs, Wasu. Have you tried creating an app for it? I bet you could sell way more eggs if you had an app!"

"An app huh?" Kuda chuckled as he shook his hung head. The conversation was getting more preposterous. He did not date much, but this reminded him of the terrible blind dates he had heard about.

"People here don't use apps like that, Tawanda. Most of these folks pay a dollar to some guy in the street to get WhatsApp downloaded onto their phone!" He hated how animated he was getting, so he drew in his breath, "Let's put a pin in this. I must get going. Are you going to eat the rest of your bread here?"

"Bread...oh the croissant? I told you you would get hungry ha! Haa, but must you run already?"

"Thanks brother," Kuda said, grabbing the half-eaten pastry in one swoop before reaching for his phantom wallet, "how much was the tea?"

"$2.50. But don't worry about it, Wasu. I got it."

"Thanks Tawanda. We'll touch base before you leave, which is?"

"This Friday morning, when could we do cof..."

"Perfect then, I'll get a hold of you before then. *Toonana*."

Chapter 8

"Younger!" Kuda hollered as he walked past the paperboy again, tossing him the half-eaten croissant as he did.

"*Aah bho, big man!*" the paperboy exclaimed and gave a thumbs up to Kuda, but the erstwhile benefactor was already in the wind, scarf now wrapped around his waist.

His heart weighed heavy. But did it weigh so because he went to meet with Tawanda guarded, or was it because of how they had actually done coffee? Had to be the latter, no?

The whole ordeal had been strange. Performative even. From the time he got there. No, from the time he invited him to do coffee at Beanster.

Was it possible that Tawanda did not remember he and Maria being particularly acquainted back when? There is no way.

By now, Kuda's pensive stride had transformed into a frantic jog. He tended to run, almost subconsciously, whenever his nerves got the best of him.

And the perfect story of how they ended up together, ha! The coward had not dared to mention getting kicked out of Maria's house by her father, the pregnancy, the miscarriage, and hastily assembled ceremony! He was sure he had not been supposed to know this, but Kuda had caught whispers of it. Parts of it anyway.

He stopped short, and immediately felt ashamed, as if he had just yelled all his thoughts to his cousin. Why was he calling Tawanda a coward? And why was he so angry?

He made a point to unclench his jaw.

What about this job though? Internship. What does that mean? "She feels like your life is not going anywhere," ah! Where is it supposed to be going? I am living until I am dead, that's it. I don't ask for food off anybody's plate. I sleep under my own roof, leaky as it may be. And where is everyone going with their lives that I am not? Is it overseas? Is our destination overseas? Maiguru has been lonely since her husband died, where is her life going? And why is Tawanda so far from home, away from his lonely mother? Ha! I stop by to see his mother once or twice a week, with my life that is not going anywhere! Where is the father of Ruramisai's child? Where did his life go? Nobody knows. Where is her life going?

He felt ashamed again. He hated himself for speaking ill of his aunt and Ruramisai, even to himself.

An app to sell chickens and eggs. Ha ha! What is this, suburban America? People have been selling eggs here since before Mbuya Nehanda. If you throw a stone anywhere here, you will likely hit someone selling eggs. For the price of airtime in Zimbabwe, you think *ma rasta* and *vana gogo* will start using some app? Nonsense.

He unclenched his jaw again, before he realised that he had been on the verge of tears.

He was home. He hung up his scarf and put away his shoes.

Chapter 9

The leak had only got worse.

He stared at the hole in the ceiling for what seemed to be hours, as he now did each morning.

The landlord was seldom around, and this hardly bothered Kuda. It gave him some leeway with the rent, which came in handy often. It also meant he could never get anything fixed, unless he wanted to do it himself.

He did not.

He had since grown a perhaps perverse comfort from the rainwater dripping onto the edge of his bed. It was an experience distinct to him and his domain.

Lately, however, there had been unsettling murmurs about the tenants getting evicted. The building had been bought by some people. Or was it due to be knocked down? The latter made more sense, Kuda mused. He had even seen the landlord twice or so around the building this month. It was twice or so more than was typical.

It had been four months since Tawanda and Maria left. Since then, Mai Tawanda had sat Kuda down to reiterate just how nowhere his life was going, encouraging him to take up his cousin's offer. Tawanda had also called him. He never called him.

Since then, Kuda's life had continued to go nowhere, as it were, at the same direction and speed that it had been going nowhere when Tawanda brought it to his attention.

Kurauone, his yesteryear friend from Watsomba, had called him a few weeks ago. He, too, never called him. Unlike Tawanda though, it was not for a lack of desire, time, or things to talk about: Kurauone and Kuda could talk for hours on end. Kurauone never had airtime and, even if he did, the network in his rural home was painstakingly unreliable.

Kuda had thus been pleasantly surprised when Kurauone not only called him, but sounded as clear as if he had been in the next room. He was calling from Marange, a regional town not too far from Watsomba. Ten years or so ago, alluvial diamonds had been discovered there, which led to thousands of people descending upon the tiny town, hoping to get in on the artisanal mining industry that had erupted. The diamond rush was illegal, and often unsafe, but it came ten years into unmitigated economic collapse across the country: people had fled to hostile lands across treacherous terrains and resorted to all manner of misconvention to survive; this was but just another desperate bid to survive.

Kurauone had resisted going to Marange for as long as he could, living off the piece of land his parents had left for him. A little after the diamonds had been discovered, the government sent the military to Marange to curb the illegal mining. And curb they did—in the only way that the Zimbabwean military curbs even the mildest of societal discord: dogs, sjamboks, gunshots onto the miners' camps from helicopters. Murmurs had it that the soldiers even had a torture camp on site. Murmurs had it that, beyond law and order, people high up in government had promised the diamonds to friends from lands far away, so were determined to keep them out of the hands of pesky Zimbabweans. It was all too much for Kurauone.

Drought in some years, and Cyclone-induced floods in others, had however compromised his most recent yields and resolve. Two years ago, the last time Kuda had seen him, Kurauone had got married and, a few months ago, had a daughter. Hands now tied, he gave in and made the short trek east.

It was from whence he had called. Apparently, things had mellowed out since the early days; the military maintained a more peripheral presence now, as many of the illegal miners had moved on to other pastures. If Kuda needed a break from the big city, Kurauone had proposed amidst chuckles, perhaps he could join him in Marange. It would be good for them to work side by side for once in their adulthood.

Kuda had said he would keep it in mind, although he had no real intention of revisiting the proposal. He was, however, headed downtown to the same construction company for which he had worked the previous year. He had received a text that they had started on a few new projects around town, and were looking for some manpower. He had not minded it the last time.

He had just got up to prepare to head downtown when there was a knock on the door.

It was the landlord.

"Comrade, how are you? Erh, I am sure you may have heard the gossip. The building must come down, city government orders. They're saying it comes down mid-August, so everyone has to be out by July. Three months comrade. In the meantime, get your back rent in order..."

Kuda nodded his head stoically, before closing the door in the befuddled landlord's face. Almost everyone he had spoken to had either been surprised by the news and timeline or had a visceral reaction to the callous request for back rent during the announcement that they had to move from this dump almost immediately.

Kuda was less perturbed, if jaded. He knew he was not going to pay the rent, and he had hardly any furnishing to worry about moving. While he had come to love his apartment, leak and all, he knew he would learn to love wherever his head laid next soon enough.

Today, however, he had a job to get to.

Chapter 10

"O sweet irony," Kuda chuckled to himself as he and the other men hopped onto the back of the pickup truck and learnt of their worksite for the day. It was at the Beanster shopping mall; a full year since he had worked there and a few months since he and Tawanda had done coffee. In place of his scarf and shoes, he now wore an ugly orange vest, helmet, and worn steel-toe boots.

None of which had meant much to him as he worked quietly under the mellow mid spring sun. Three hours into his shift, however, he had to use the bathroom. He decided to take his chances at Beanster. They did not look too busy. Besides, he recognised the security guard; it was the same one who had called him "Sir." Kuda walked past him with an exaggerated smile and subtle nod. As he got to the door, he heard the guard yell out,

"*Hey wena!* Where are you going?"

"Agh boss. Why are you being loud? I am just going to use the toilet!"

"Ah ah. What's wrong with you people? You think this is a public toilet?"

"No, I…" Kuda stared at the man. Where affected respect had once stood, now stood condescending disdain. The man tilted his head slightly, wondering from where he recognised this man, oblivious to the social and professional mores of bathroom usage at high-end places. He decided that he had never before seen him, and ordered him away from Beanster with raised voice and wagging finger.

Wry smile returned to Kuda's face, before turning around and dragging his feet across the coffee shop and into the parking lot in slow, deliberate defiance.

Kuda let out a manic chuckle as he walked away. He almost felt sorry for the guard. He had seen the look in his eyes before. Osama. Tawanda. He had always thought that their eyes spit on his lowly self. He now wondered if it was something else. If it had anything at all to do with him.

Pathetic.

"Big Man!"

The high-pitched yelp broke Kuda's musings. It was the paperboy. By now, Kuda was walking past him, rapt in thought. The boy extended his fist in gleeful greeting.

"*Bho here mudhara!* Jah Bless!"

Kuda reciprocated the fist pump, extending his smile in recognition of the boy's homage. Like the other people in the parking lot, the boy would have heard, or at least seen, his intended humiliation. He would have remembered him, too, as the man with the scarf, the shoes, and the croissant. Now in a vest and helmet.

Yet here he was, still.

He had seen the look in his eyes before. Kurauone. Maria.

Chapter 11

He was going to miss the leak.

By now, Kuda had got rid of everything that constituted furniture in his apartment, save for the mattress and hot plate. He had been able to get three dollars for his iron, but the rest had not been much in resale value. Between the three dollars, and the five he had received from Tawanda back then and had since forgotten about, meant he had just enough for the bus.

He still had two weeks before the apartment building had to be vacated, but he had decided not to wait until then. He had not worked in almost a month, and the constant limbo had worn him down. Perhaps his life was not going anywhere, after all. He would leave within the week.

Two weeks ago, he called Kurauone, hoping he was still at the mines. Maybe he could tell him what to do. Kurauone always knew what he should do.

"Chief *wepa*Salisbury! *Madiiko?*" Kurauone had picked up with much aplomb, which gave Kuda a hearty laugh. Although Kuda hardly laughed lately, one could always count on Kurauone to get him going.

"*Bho mumwe wangu!* How are you? What are the diamonds talking about?

"Ha! They are saying "when is your friend joining us? Haha!"

"Ah! Haha. So, I guess it's not bad huh!"

"Not bad? *Eish,* it is not easy comrade, but when it is good, it is good. My man, when I tell you that Loveness's fees are taken care of, just from one rock I found last week!"

"Yeah?"

"Truth, comrade. In fact, I am planning on going back home in the next two weeks. The little that I have come by should last the family through the winter. Then we will see…"

"Ah ah! It is in order then. Haa. Ko *ma*gunners, how far? Are they not causing problems anymore?"

"*Eish, ipapo manje.* They are…around. They fall back and wait for the kill; they are not hunting like they used to! You just have to be clever. The youths here have made a whole *zhet* of being on lookout. System, boss. System! hehe."

"Haa bho then. Two weeks? *Eish.*"

"What were you saying?"

"Haa comrade. The big city has been a monster recently. You know me, I'm not the crying crying type. But haa. I don't know. I thought maybe I could come and see whether you are telling the truth or not. I know you and your stories, Kura,

65

haha!" To Kurauone, the tapered laughing ill-concealed his best friend's fatigued uncertainty.

"Hah! Is Chief from the capital ready to slum it with us commoners! Haa yes *mhani*. Okay. So me, let me not leave just yet then. Get here, settle in, then I will make the Watsomba move."

"Haa Kura *sha*. Don't stick around on my account, I will figure it out when I get there…"

"Are you joking? It's a jungle out here, haha! You will need me to show you one or two ropes! But haa, more importantly, it would be good to catch up, heh! And that way, I can take to Watsomba whatever you bring for Gogo, and of course, your niece Loveness, ha ha!"

"*Eish*. I have no words, *mumwe wangu*. So, cool. I will plan to be there on the tenth. That is three weeks, give or take. We will finalise details closer to the date."

"Listen to this guy! "Finalise the date," haha! Okay Mr. Big City! Call me anytime. I am usually up late back by the camps where there is better network, so any time is teatime! Let me go back to the fields, see what harvest lay before us today."

"*Bho saka*. Talk soon."

That was two weeks ago. Kuda had now decided not to wait the full three weeks, as discussed earlier. There was nothing here.

A drop fell on his head. He smiled as he got up from the old mattress for the last time.

He shoved all his clothes into a giant *saga*-bag, and the hotplate, and a few plates into a small box. Let the rats and homeless have his old mattress, if they could get there before the Great Fall. Ha! He was going to spend the night at Maiguru Mai Tawanda's, before catching the bus to Marange early the following morning. That way, he could turn the key for the apartment in today, and make sure he bid his aunt farewell.

As he stood by the door, Kuda felt a groundswell of sadness in his stomach. He stroked the door gently for a moment, before slamming it behind him and darting towards the Landlord's office. *Saga*-bag on his back and box under his arm, Kuda more closely resembled a released prisoner than a tenant leaving his home of a few years. To the rest of the world, anyway. The neighbours understood. There was an air of escape from the apartment building. So they stood by their windows, applauding whoever among them was moving out before doomsday. People who had not spoken to each other in years enthusiastically volunteered to help each other load furniture onto trucks or carry it to the bus.

Kuda obviously did not need the help. He dropped the key in the Landlord's mailbox and set on his way, deaf to the cheers of his now yester neighbours. He had, in the beginning, been motivated by his desire to leave. The old building...the city...his life that was not going anywhere. But now, he was getting...excited. What if he found a rock right away? Even if it took him a month. He was bound to find something. Kurauone had sounded hopeful! Oh Kura. Oh, to be working alongside his friend. He had not felt this way in ages. Perhaps not since high school.

He decided to call Kurauone. Chat with him as he walked to his aunt's place, making arrangements for his arrival and to while the time away. His friend did not pick up. He was probably down in the mines. In any case, Marange phone network was unreliable, Kurauone always said. It did not matter. He was one sleep away from the land of diamonds. Ha!

Chapter 12

He could tell that Maiguru was avoiding his gaze since he got there. She busied herself with every chore in the house while he sat in the living room. This was unlike her. She never compromised on the ritual of sitting down for formal greetings and offering of food, regardless of how informal or familiar the guest was. After twenty minutes that, to Kuda, had seemed like the whole night, she called out to him, "Kuda *mwanangu*! Come help me with this firewood."

"*Bho mhamha*, here I come," he called back, making haste to get outside. She had sounded more like she was summoning him to court than seeking his help, yet even that was preferable to the ominous stillness inside.

After a few minutes of him swinging the axe and her taking the resulting logs to a fire she had started, she finally broke the silence.

"Do you remember Baba naMai Maria, Tawanda's in-laws?"

He nodded, smiling ruefully as he remembered doing coffee with Tawanda. She continued, "Well, once upon a time, perhaps before you moved to the city, we were thick as thieves, your uncle and I and them two. *Tsono neshinda*. Then some nonsense happened. I will spare you the details, but we drifted because of it. It was only when they left that they had started to reach out again, but your uncle died not too long after. Even with Tawa and Maria's union, things still don't feel right. The gripe was with Baba, and he left before they—we finished our issues."

"Eish. That's rough *mhamha*," Kuda responded, transfixed on the fire as he wrestled between asking her for more details on the nonsense and waiting to hear where she was going with her parable.

"Things are to be said while we are still here. There is no reconciliation from beyond the grave. You know, my son. When I said your life was not going anywhere, I did not mean…"

"*Aiwa Maiguru*. I know. But you were right. This isn't living! This is me just whiling time until I die. Might as well go while it away where each day comes with a bit of hope. Were it not so, would all those people have flocked there?"

"*Iwe* Kudakwashe! What manner of talk is that? You want to bring the spirit of death into my house!? Besides, we did not spend all that money sending you to school so you could become some filthy, illegal miner!

"Sorry mother. I did not mean it like that," Kuda answered, coyly looking down. "I was just saying…perhaps it is time to try something else."

"Something else like this? This is your something else? If we are doing any old illegal thing, why don't you become a robber like these other children with no sense then?"

"*Nhai Maiguru*. You know this is not like that at all."

"No, I don't know. How would I know? All I know is it's illegal, it's for goons, and the government is cracking down. Do you never watch the news? Also, you have that offer from Tawanda's workplace overseas. Marange or Maryland: how is this even a debate? I thought you were smarter than this, Kudakwashe!"

The last part grieved Kuda's spirit into silence. Over the years, he had grown impervious to most injury and insult. Annoyed, indeed, but he would soon get over it. He, however, still could not bear to have his intelligence questioned. That was the line those close to him never dared to cross: well, most people close to him. This instance hurt that much more, not only because Maiguru knew this chink in his armour well, but because Tawanda was the smart place. All his life charting a path for himself in the shadows, only to end up here: where the best decision his jealously guarded intelligence was supposed to make would find him interning for his cousin. Rock bottom.

"*Eish Maiguru*. It's getting late. I must wake up and shut the rooster's mouth tomorrow. Your words, I have heard. I will go do two weeks or so, clear my mind in the process. We can pick up where we left off when I get back…"

"Ah, pick up what? I have said what I have to say! If you leave tomorrow, then don't bother…" Maiguru caught herself, but her retort and its intended direction were not lost on her nephew.

"You are sleeping without eating?" she continued in a whisper, masking her own tears with the rising smoke.

"It's okay, mother of mine. I'll see you at dawn."

Maiguru did not answer, allowing the smoke to trouble her eyes in a hastily established self-imposed penance ritual. Kuda stood for a few moments, waiting for one of them to speak first. He turned, forlorn, went back into the house and made for bed.

Chapter 13

Kuda could not sleep.

Between the anxiety of pending travel and the heavy words from Maiguru, he had many a thought to keep him company for the night. He stared at the ceiling, yearning for the familiar leaking. It tolled the bell to his erstwhile kingdom. Now, the silence exposed him. His weakness. Vulnerability. Life that was not going anywhere. The morning seemed days away and, even then, he would be waking up to a futile morrow.

What had Maiguru meant to say? That if he left, he could not come back there? That stung him. He did not even live there! He had left home before she had ever asked him to; before many of his peers left their parents' house.

He got up a little after midnight and dug around his bag for his notebook. He had not written in or even opened it for a few months. But he had for such a time as this. He started to write. He wrote about the conversation with Maiguru earlier that night. He wrote about the past few months. Tawanda and Maria's visit. The birthday party and doing coffee. He wrote about Kurauone and how he would be with him at the diamond mines soon. Tomorrow! He flipped through the pages to when he had started writing in the now-slightly tattered book. It was soon after he had moved to Harare. The new school. Osama and the Taliban. O, how he had been both angry and scared back then. He chuckled to himself. He liked that he could chuckle about it now. Maria. Watsomba. Gogo. I swear, if I was somebody who mattered, they would pay thousands for this book. Put it in a museum even. Hah! This old, tattered thing in the museum.

He checked the time again. Two thirty in the morning. Just as well. He needed to be at the bus station at five if he was going to be in Marange by noon. He showered quietly and, realising he was hungry from not having eaten the previous night, snuck into the kitchen. He was surprised to see that Maiguru had prepared a feast. Rice, oxtail, salad. It was the sort of dinner she used to make when Babamukuru was still here. He was a good man. She had even packed some for Kuda to take with him! She put it in the same yellow-lid lunch boxes that he, Tawanda, and Ruramisai had used back in high school. He could not believe she still had them. He could not believe she had done all this for him, especially given their fight the night before. Was it a fight? Well, whatever it was, she had been upset. She would be fine. He will be back soon. Maybe with a small fortune.

He would leave at 4am, he decided. He would just wake his aunt then to bid her farewell.

That way, he did not disturb her much, and spare them both a prolonged awkward goodbye. To while the time away, he turned on the television and scrolled, listless, through the football highlights. He had, once upon a time, loved the game. He, Tawanda, and Babamukuru used to make a weekend out of watching the games back in simpler times. Oftentimes, it was the only thing around which they had come together as ritual. It seemed such a distant memory now. He had lost interest after Babamukuru died and Tawanda left. He had stopped watching all together when he moved out of Maiguru's house. He tried to remember the last full game he had watched, but immediately gave up the pursuit. He tried to remember what had filled the football-sized hole in his life since the last time he had watched. Nothing enjoyable, or worthwhile, came to his mind. He felt sorry for who he had become. Yet, even as he felt sorry, he felt detached from the pitiful Kuda of his musings; as if the person for whom he felt sorry was an erstwhile stranger.

3:30am.

He decided to try Kurauone again. He was typically up at this time, and by better phone network, he had told him. Again, the phone rang. Hah! Trust Kurauone to brag about how late he stayed awake, only to fall asleep anyway. He had always meant well, but often either overstated his abilities or underestimated responsibilities. That was just him though. Kuda was excited to see him later that day. Today.

He went to wake his aunt up five minutes before four. His anxiety had gotten the best of him. To his surprise, she was already up, sitting in bed with her rosary in hand. She had been crying.

"Good morning, mother. I was going to take my leave now."

She shook her head slightly without ever lifting it, then spoke raspily, "Okay *mwanangu*. If this is what you have so desired… Be safe. Did you see the food?"

"Yes Maiguru. Thank you very much, this will hold me up until the weekend," Kuda said with a nervous chuckle, attempting to inject some levity into the air. Maiguru remained stoic.

"If it's all the same with you, *mwanangu*, I won't get up to see you out. I have work in tw…"

"*Aiwa* Maiguru! Not at all. I am all packed and ready; you would be making me late, hehe. I will catch a taxi by the gate there. Those guys are up with the witches, ha!"

"Okay, Kuda…God and those gone before us be with you."

"*Mazvita* Maiguru. Stay well, and God willing, I will see you soon."

He could not have got out of there soon enough. Between the residual tension from the previous night, his excitement, and Maiguru's half slumber, the conversation had been miserable.

He grabbed his bag and, crudely fitting the lunchbox into its side pocket, dashed out of the house like a fugitive of its demons. He did not wait for long outside. Just as he had imagined, the first taxis were passing by, and he caught the first one he saw. It was already full to the brim; mainly laborers hoping to get picked up for a shift. He wondered if some of them would be headed to Beanster. Ha! Maybe when he got back, he could go back there—maybe do coffee this time. Ha! By himself? That would be nice. Perhaps go on a date. Ha! He had not thought about women in a long time, it seemed. It may be time now. If things start looking up from here…

His phone rang. It was Kurauone. His friend always had terrible timing, he mused to himself. Kuda never answered his phone on public transport unless he absolutely had to. In addition to it being generally frowned upon among passengers of public transit, he also despised having to raise his voice and, more importantly, the feeling that people were listening or watching him. He would call him back when he got to the station.

Kurauone called again, prompting annoyed glances from one or two of the passengers, and Kuda put his phone on silent. Now, where was he? Ah, Beanster.

He barely had time to pick up where his mind had left him before realising he was already at the station. Just as well. He was not sure he wanted to go back to Beanster, even in his daydreams.

He jumped out of the taxi with the same sense of manufactured agency with which he had left the house. One bus to Mutare was almost full already, and he thought of just getting on that one. He was, however, early, and wanted to make sure he got himself a good seat. Besides, he needed a moment to call his friend back. There was another, much emptier bus that was only starting to load passengers. The conductor was not even screaming at passers-by to board yet. He walked towards that one, much to the chagrin of the other conductor. He found a seat all to himself, at least for now.

As he dug through his bag for his notebook, his phone rang again. Ah. Kurauone! In his rush to get to the bus, he had forgotten to call his friend back. Just as well he had not got on that earlier bus; his friend would have been calling him non-stop on the bus!

"Hello Kura! Haha you impatient man! Sorry we missed each oth…"

"*Makadii henyu?* This is not Kurauone*ba*." It was not Kurauone. It was a woman. A woman in unmistakable distress. "It's Mai Loveness…"

Mai Loveness? Who was Mai Loveness? It took Kuda a few seconds to remember that Loveness was the name of Kurauone's daughter. Maybe it's because he had always been Kurauone to him, or maybe because he still had not been back to Watsomba to see his friend's daughter; Kuda had still not taken to calling his friend Baba Loveness. Even more obscure to him, then, was the existence of a Mai Loveness. Indeed, Kurauone spoke endless about her, but the name remained an idea unattached to a being for now.

"Ah yes, Mai Loveness! Is everything okay? I was calling Baba Loveness back, letting him know I had started the trip."

"No that wasn't Baba Loveness calling earlier," she responded in a futile attempt to hold back tears. "It was me… Baba is dead," she was able to whisper, before letting out a piercing shriek and began to bellow. From the sound of it, she was surrounded by other people. A man came to the phone.

"Hello, *makadiiko?*"

"Hi. This is Kuda. I am Kurauone's friend, on my way to see him in Marange as we speak. Would you mind telling me what is going on?"

"*Eish, mudhara*. There was an incident last night. Gunners came out of nowhere and put three in him…"

Kuda hung up the phone. He looked around the almost empty bus, and stood up to leave. He stumbled towards the door. In a daze, he dialled Maiguru's number. She did not pick up. Must have gone back to sleep. He scrolled through his phone for someone to call. In times like this, it would be Kurauone he called. He stood with his undialled phone to his ear, expecting phantom voice to speak to him. It was then he realised he had left his bag on the bus. He stumbled back in, pushing past the growing number of passengers that had since arrived. He grabbed it and walked back two steps towards the door, turned back, and threw the bag back onto the seat, before collapsing on top of it.

Chapter 14

Kuda did not remember the rest of his trip to Marange. He may have slept on the bus. Did he? He had to be awake to change buses once he got to Mutare. He knew that much. Not that it mattered.

Now in Marange, he was greeted by a weeping Mai Loveness. Since they were children, he and Kurauone had spoken in fantasy about the women they would marry. Now he was meeting Kurauone's wife. Except, instead of Kurauone doing the introductions, she was doing them herself underneath a flood of tears. Not how they had dreamt it those many moons ago.

A man from the mine compound was with Mai Loveness. He was the same man who had taken the phone from her when she had called Kuda earlier. He had introduced himself, but Kuda had failed to hold on to the name. This was very unlike him; he prided himself in remembering names. Leaving a weeping Mai Loveness by herself under the shade of a baobab tree, the man grabbed Kuda by the hand and walked him away from her hearing.

The rumour mill had been abuzz since Kurauone's death, the man explained to Kuda. As such, he had stitched together a decent, if sickening, account of the night's events from some of the other miners who had been at or near the site on that day.

Kurauone had decided to stay at the mines into the evening. While a decent-sized cohort would often work beyond sundown, most of the men and women would leave by then. Not only was it harder to see, and torches would draw unwanted attention, but the soldiers were also known to descend about the site more commonly and brutally under the dark of night than during the day. Kurauone was among the majority that typically left early.

Over the past two weeks, however, he had started to stay a bit later each day, the man explained. He said his friend would be joining him at the mines and was hoping to take it easy with him for a few days after he arrived: if he worked harder now and possibly scored a rock, he could afford to do that. Others had warned him to be careful. Not only was there a higher chance of being caught by the police or soldiers, but the other men who worked late had developed a militant camaraderie and were generally hostile towards anyone who joined their late-night parties. While they could not outright tell people not to come, it was well understood. If one such miner was to get lucky and the men found out, he would almost certainly be robbed before the night was over.

On this evening, the man continued, Kurauone had been working a small patch close to the fence. He was doing his best to stay away from the rest of the men in a ceremonial bid to heed the warnings he had received. Knee-deep into washing off some rocks, the other men began whistling. No yelling, just whistling. Kurauone stood alert, fearing that this may be code to attack him. He faced the direction where the rest of the men were working, expecting to see them coming his way. Being close to the fence, he was confident he would outrun them if needed. To his surprise, the men seemed to be running, cautiously in different directions; all but towards him. He then froze, statuesque, likely trying to decipher the sudden burning along his back, followed by a kick to the back of his legs that brought him to his knees.

That was the last the rest of the men had seen him—alive, anyway. They had returned to the site two hours later and found a most macabre sight. Kurauone's body hung lifeless on top of the barbed wire fence, his right eye having popped out of its socket. He had been so badly beaten that, had the other men not had their eye on him the previous night and seen the soldiers get to him, he would not have been easily identified. Word had got round the compound that some of the late-night miners, the most rogue of their bunch, had thrown up upon discovering the mangled body. In what sweet redemption there may be to such a gruesome scene, it appeared that Kurauone had been mercifully finished off by a bullet to the back of the head.

Kuda could not decide whether he appreciated the man's detailed account, or if he hated him for it. For now, he had to make arrangements to take his friend back to Watsomba.

Chapter 15

He changed the channel again. "The Good, the Bad, The Ugly" was on. Not that it mattered to him; his eyes merely glazed over the screen long enough to notice what was on before he changed it again. He barely noticed Maiguru, who sat on the couch across from him.

It had been three weeks since Kuda returned to Harare. He and Mai Loveness had taken Kurauone from Marange to be buried in Watsomba. They had thrown his friend, covered in a worn blanket, onto the top of a bus in the sweltering late winter sun. Kuda had the indignity suffered by his friend's body with every jolt that came as the hardened bus meandered the stony rural dust roads. *Vintage Kurauone. Always had the luck of one whose ancestors were the village drunks. The one time his notoriously homebound self decided to venture out, he returns home in an old blanket on top of a bus. The one night he decides to stay up later at the worksite, the soldiers descend upon the mines.*

Kuda had returned to Harare, head held lower than any time before he left the city. He came to Maiguru's gate like the prodigal son and, true to the tale, she embraced him as he did. Not a word was mentioned about their earlier squabbles. Just as well, for Kuda was haunted enough. He obsessed over the sight of Kurauone's mangled body. He found himself unwittingly coming back to the image. Indeed, his friend had been cleaned up before he finally saw him, but it was still gruesome. When he had been returned to Watsomba, only the men of the village had been allowed to see him before the burial: it was decided that this was no way for the women and children to remember him.

When Kuda was not remembering Kurauone battered and lifeless in the coffin, he was imagining him hung over the fence, as the man had described him. He felt guilt. Guilty for the obsessive regression to the horror at each turn. Why was he thus fascinated? He considered that, on another day, a week or two from his arrival in Watsomba, it could have been him on that fence. He felt guilty because Kurauone was there because of him. He would have left for Watsomba earlier if Kuda had never committed to coming. He should have just gone to America, where Tawanda and Maiguru wanted him. He mused over the man's retelling. Kurauone had stayed up late that night, again, on account of his pending arrival. He felt guilty that it wasn't him mangled atop that fence. Perhaps it should have. He had no Mai Loveness to come home to. No Loveness. He was just a shell of a man, with a life that was not going anywhere. Even when he tried, he met a dead end. A dead end, hah! He stopped short. He felt guilty for making this about himself. Woe be Kuda! His best friend died, yet he was still worse off than him! Pathetic either way: whether he felt guilty or fortunate for having dodged the bullet, after the beating, of course.

Maiguru had been tender. She reminded him of when he first got to Harare from Watsomba, a decade and some ago. She seemingly stayed out of his way, only coming around to announce she was leaving or that the food was ready. Tawanda called to check in with him once every couple of days; about as many times as he typically called in a year. Ruramisai stopped by every now and then as well. Short of Babamukuru, Kuda felt some semblance of family in the city for the first time in years. He did not know what to do with that feeling.

"*Mwanangu*," Maiguru broke through the vapid air of the living room, "I was trying to wait until you were ready, but I know how grief goes; it offers no timetable…"

Kuda stared straight at the television, which he had now muted.

Maiguru continued, "So please, do not take this as me trying to hurry you along in any direction; you are welcome to stay here as long as you need to. But I was talking to Tawanda, and he told me to remind you that the offer for America was still on the table. So, something to just thi…"

"I'll do it."

"Oh?" was all Maiguru could muster. She was surprised. She had not expected him to be this eager. Given how militantly he had dodged the idea the last time they had the conversation, she was hardly expecting him to even consider it. He had thus stumped her.

"Yeah. What do I have to stay for? I am just a shell of a man here. Nothing to show. Even Kurauone had Mai Loveness weeping for him. Had me to take him home. He lives on in Loveness. I could literally fall off the face of the earth today, and nobo..." he cast a glance at his aunt and saw her discomfort. Kuda felt bad. As justified as he felt in his despondency, Maiguru had done nothing to be counted as "nobody." But while he valued her maternal sympathies, he got no comfort from knowing that the only person he could now count upon was someone who had bound themselves to care for him since his adolescence. To him, it was a stark reminder that he had put nothing into the world that made people care about him. Kurauone had been that person. Now, he was not.

Maiguru may have been pained, but she understood. Kuda stopped his descent into self-pity and, with affected optimism, continued, "So yes! States may be just what I need. Get a new start in...where does Tawanda live again? It doesn't matter, Marymount or something. Put in that work, as they say out there! Hah!"

"It is well then… Next time I talk to Tawanda I will let him know how you are thinking."

"Thank you Maiguru. He has called me a few times too since I got back; we'll get to working on it."

Chapter 16

"Okay Cuzzo. Say what's up to the missus!" Kuda exclaimed as he got off the phone with Tawanda. Overhearing half the conversation from the kitchen, Maiguru smiled. She could not remember a time when Kuda had sounded like this. Maybe high school? He sounded excited. Hopeful. Happy even.

She was not far off. Kuda remained cautious of feeling happy, lest life pull the rug from under his feet as it tended to do. It was now January, and the last five months had provided rays of light in a desolate season. Since returning to Harare, and especially after beginning to plan to leave, Kuda and Maiguru grew closer than they had ever been. Kuda loosened long-held inhibitions about not being her son in a world in which her actual son sometimes acted as if Kuda did not exist.

Maiguru finally let herself enjoy companionship in the house again for the first time after Babamukuru died, Tawanda left, and Ruramisai and Kuda moved out. Word of Kuda's pending departure had got to Gogo and, for the first time in decades, she left Watsomba and, by bus, came to spend the Christmas holiday in Harare. Plans were moving along for the trip. If all went well, Tawanda explained, Kuda could start his internship at the beginning of May. Since they would not be paying him right away, the partners had also agreed to pay for his ticket. Just as well then, he thought. He had saved up a few dollars from his eggs and odd jobs that he had thought would go towards the ticket. Maiguru had promised to chip in with a few hundred dollars as well. That money could now go towards getting him settled once he got there. He could make the trip at the beginning of April and spend the month getting to know the area. And help around the house too, now that Maria was pregnant. Oh, Maria was pregnant now too, Tawanda had tacked on to the end of one of their conversations.

Kuda was even excited about that news. It will be a season of rejuvenation all around! Poor Maiguru; all by herself again! Perhaps he could convince Ruramisai to move back in with her. Listen to me, Kuda chuckled to himself. He had never felt any real agency when it came to family; except maybe when it came to Gogo. What change having something to look forward to can inspire. This is what prisoners on the verge of release must feel like. He was uncomfortable with the prisoner analogy, so he tried again. This is what the president-elect, on the verge of taking office, must feel like. Not like the president here though, hah! A real, elected president, in America for example. He hated himself for deriding his homeland. He had always resented that talk, which seemed to roll off the tongues of Tawanda and others who had left or spent their entire lives wanting to leave with ease. This place had taken everything he had though. It may not have been much to begin with, but he had things. He had his decent book smarts, which had amounted to nothing. The street smarts he had had to develop otherwise were only good for keeping him alive, and barely that. He had friends. Not many, but he had them. Maria. Kurauone. This place had taken them both. He had memories; memories that may now always be bookmarked by one he had not even seen: a man mangled in the barbed wire fence.

He had a leak in the roof. He had even lost that. He had a scarf and nice shoes. Oh, his scarf and shoes! He had not thought about them in months. They made him smile. He would take them with him to the USA. They were probably stylish, even by American standards, hah! He wondered if the prisoner awaiting release and the president awaiting inauguration felt the same anxieties as him. As each other?

Chapter 17

He packed up his recently purchased suitcase and weighed it on Maiguru's bathroom scale. 15 Kilograms. Good. Well below the required 23 at the airport. With a grin atypical of him across his face, he paced towards the door, dragging the suitcase behind with all the air of a high-rolling businessman. Then, with a gleeful spin, he turned and headed back to the bedroom.

This little routine had become a daily ritual for Kuda. It was only the early days of March, but he had packed and unpacked the bag a dozen times already. He would decide on taking something with him, then decide against it. Maiguru had also told him to leave space for some high school memorabilia Tawanda had asked her to send with him when he travelled. It did not matter much to him if 20 of the kilograms ended up being parcels for Tawanda and Maria. And their baby. Uncle Kuda. Hah! He was an uncle already by way of Ruramisai, and he cherished that role. He would, however, be the American baby's Zimbabwean uncle, and the only one at that. It would be nice being that person; Lord knows Tawanda and Maria could not wait to forget about Zimbabwe, he chuckled to himself.

Kuda tampered his excitement. He felt...nervous. Was this nervous? The last time he remembered feeling nervous was when he moved to Harare to start high school. But those nerves had overwhelmingly felt terrible. He shuddered even in reminiscing about them. These new nerves were bearable. He was not afraid. He was just anxious to get going.

He wondered what America he would arrive in. He had seen all types of America on TV, the cinema, and books since he was a child. The cowboys with lassos. America of the Westerns. The Suburban America of the Fresh Prince. The hip-hop America of the music videos. The one Osama and his friends had tried so hard to mimic back in high school. Hah! Osama. He had not thought about him in years. He never thought of it then, but now chuckled at how a Zimbabwean kid calling himself Osama had devoted his life to appearing as American as possible. Kuda wondered if Osama had ever made it to his beloved America after all. If he ever "dropped rhymes" or whatever in Harlem? O, sweet irony that *Wasu* would now be in America, and Osama is wherever he is. Probably not America though! Life has a way of doing these things. Nobody is bigger than it, Kuda chuckled again.

He remembered something he meant to ask Tawanda about the next time he called. He had heard on the news that there was a virus. He had only sort of listened while he packed, so he could not remember it all. *But it was like the Swine Flu. Remember that? Whatever happened to that? These people and all these diseases. What was that one a few years ago- Ziko, Zika? But anyway, this one started in China. People eating bats or something. Crazy!*

In Watsomba, he had known some people who ate mice. *That was not too far from bats, was it? Still, bats look so evil, don't they? How could…ah, God and his people! Different, different. They probably think we are strange too, huh. Apparently, it was now in America. Corona, I think they're calling it. Corona! What a strange name for it. In Shona, korona means crown. Well, it's not really Shona, is it?* He had taken a Latin class in high school and, although he did not remember much of it, he remembered that corona also meant crown. We probably got it from there. *So what, is this the king of diseases? Ha ha! We'll see how it goes. You never know with these things!*

His train of thought was interrupted by Maiguru tapping gently, almost meekly, on the bedroom door. Just as well.

"Ah Maiguru! What's up?" He welcomed her with a puerile glee that would have been uncharacteristic at any other point in his story prior to the past two months or so.

"I'm fine," she responded, as timid as she had knocked. This was very much outside of their most recent rambunctious rapport, "I just got off the phone with Tawanda…"

Kuda's heart sank. Something had happened, he could just tell. "Is he okay? The baby…"

"No, no," Maiguru said, with a feeble chuckle, "They're okay. But I don't know if you've been paying attention to the news; this Coronavirus 19 thing…"

He thought his heart had sunk earlier. It had not. Now, it did.

"He says not to worry too much; there's just been a minor change of plans. They still want you to come, the company does. But because they do not know what this disease will mean for their business, fiscal year what what, they're not able to pay for the flight anymore. But…" Maiguru made haste to continue before Kuda got any more despondent., "as the ancestors would have it, I had set a bit aside still; you never know what's going to happen."

Life returned to Kuda's eyes like a baby at play. Utter relief. Out of necessity, and repeated assurances from Tawanda that he would be covered, he had spent the little money he had saved to contribute to the ticket on the new bag and a few other things. Maiguru, as only vintage Maiguru would do, had thought ahead. The Coronavirus murmurs had unsettled her. Pulling from her savings and the meagre amounts she got from Babamukuru's pension, she had a few dollars ready to make sure Kuda went away to start his new life, come what may.

"Ah, *nhai* Mother of mine! What do you want me to do? How do I thank you?" Kuda said as if reciting a praise poem, mimicking a swaying dance most synonymous with older women thanking their children. Maiguru chuckled as she left the room.

Chapter 18

Kuda sat on the bed, playing a game on his phone with his legs stretched out over his packed suitcase. As his departure drew nearer, what nerves there may have been a few weeks ago were now gone. *Not gone like he was no longer worried. Gone like he had worried as much as he could and lost feeling in his nerves. A man about to be thrown into a den of lions lays sleepless for days before his fate,* Kuda mused. *But surely, as he marches towards the inevitable on the day of reckoning, his heart is probably at the most ease it has felt in recent times, no?* This is perhaps where he was now. Once more, when the lion eventually pounces, his heart may beat right out of his chest, but for now, he sat in stoic resignation. He smirked at his choice of analogy. Why were his analogies always gruesome? He could have spoken of the nerves of someone who was about to start a new job, get married, or have a child, and the metaphor would have made the same, or similar sense. If anything, was this far more akin to a rebirth than it was to certain death?

His internal debate was interrupted by his phone ringing. Tawanda. It had been a while since he had last spoken to him; perhaps two weeks now? Not a long time on the grander scale, but Tawanda had been calling routinely, at least once a week, over the past few months. All was in order though; any messages that needed passing on could be passed on through Maiguru, as had been the one about the tickets a week and a half ago.

"Big bro!" Kuda answered with such high-pitched glee that even surprised him. It probably surprised Tawanda too. Kuda could not be sure though, as his cousin replied in uncharacteristically sombre voice. Uncharacteristic most times, but especially so given their recent rapport.

"Hey Kuda, how are you doing?"

This un-numbed Kuda's lion's den-bound nerves.

"I am well. What's up?" he responded, recoiling back into the impermeable stolid shell he had crafted so diligently over the years, only shedding it ever so slightly in recent months.

"Listen. I'm not going to beat around the bush here. We've had to change a few things at work. This Corona thing, eish…"

"Oh no problem *mudhara*. Maiguru told me last week. Haha! Fortunately for us, she had not spent the little ticket money that she'd set asi…"

"No, I'm not talking about that Wasu," Tawanda paused. In the chasm of pregnant silence, Kuda knew. He said nothing.

"There is no telling what this whole thing is going to mean for business. They are already talking about stopping international travel. It's… We may have to suspend some operations soon. Long story long Wasu, *haaa*. The internship is off the table."

Kuda said nothing. There was much he wanted to say. To ask. Was this Tawanda's plan all along? To bring him to the cusp in excitement, only to…No. Not even he could be that cynical. But was it not presumptuous to rescind such an offer before anyone knew what this virus was going to be? We've had a dozen viruses go, well, viral, in the past two decades; who ever shut down shop because of them?

"Kuda?"

"Haa, tough break comrade. I understand. Let's see what happens. Thanks for even trying…"

"Look, man. If it all boils over and things get back to normal, we'll be sure to make this a priority, Wasu! Don't worry, I promise."

"All good, cousin. Don't sweat it. How is Maria plus one?"

Chapter 19

"Did you remember to pack the parcel with the dress? And your food?" Maiguru asked, as Kuda lumbered downstairs with his suitcase.

"Indeed Maiguru. I think that's everything."

A month had gone by since the phone call from Tawanda. It had ushered into the household yet another season of unspoken frigidity, not too dissimilar from a few months earlier.

Except this time, it was Maiguru who bore the brunt of disillusionment. The dream she had sold her nephew, no less on the heels of tragedy, had come to naught. His life was not going anywhere. The phrase haunted her. Had she put his fate into the wind when she said this? The ancestors know she meant well. Distraught, she spent her days between her bedroom and willing the maternal empathy within her bones into being in self-imposed penance.

Except this time, Kuda was at peace. If more people had known about his intended exodus, they may have been surprised at how quickly he seemed to move past it. Tawanda and Maiguru were certainly incredulous, as ones waiting for a predicted storm even as outside continues to shine. As he got off the phone that day, he had felt a familiarity that placated him right away. This was how his life went.

Could it be that some lives are not meant to go anywhere? He was almost disturbed at how calm he was.

No time to be disturbed though; Maiguru seemed to be taking the cancelled trip much harder than he was. The first week had been full of her turning herself around to make sure he did not sink further into melancholy. Having seen that he had held on to his sanity, she began her own descent. The next two weeks were full of Kuda turning himself around to make sure she did not sink further into melancholy. The last week or so had been attrition. No anger. No joy either. Just an uncomfortable peace. Two ships amiably passing each other in the depths of night, but passing each other nonetheless.

Kuda knew what he had to do. He had to return to her the sanctity of her space. He needed her to know he was okay without her feeling responsible for making sure of it. He also needed to find, or rediscover, a place before he knew that life had to go somewhere.

He had to go to Watsomba.

He did not think too much about it; just replaced the parcels that would have been for Tawanda and Maria with those that would be for Gogo in his bag. She would be happy to see him.

Today, Maiguru insisted on driving him to the bus stop. Just as well, Kuda explained, he had to stop by the Beanster shopping mall before he left. He was in no hurry; he just had some loose ends to tie up. Just as well, Maiguru said, she wanted to get some groceries for him to take to Gogo, as well as take care of some other business there while he did what he had to do. He slid twenty dollars into her back and asked if she could buy a few extra things. Baby food, diapers—how much does that cost anyway? As much as you can get on a twenty.

They drove in awkward silence for a few minutes, before they began to ask each other a question at the same time. They both chuckled, before Kuda gestured for her to go ahead.

"So, how long are you going to be gone?"

"Ah, I don't know, Maiguru. We'll see where the rod and the fruit fall, as the elders say." He felt compelled to say more, but she did not push it any further. She understood.

"And you, Maiguru? What are you going to do?"

"Eish. I'm not sure, *mwanangu*. This virus thing has thrown a wrench in the spokes, as it were. But as soon as I can travel again, I'm thinking of using that money to go help your cousin with the baby when it comes."

"That.... That's nice. That's as it should be, Maiguru, as it should be."

They nodded their heads in tandem, erstwhile smiles sneaking across both their faces.

"So, what are you doing at Beansters?"

"Oh, I just have to see one or two old friends."

Maiguru glanced at him through the corner of her eye. He had no friends that he would absolutely have to see before he left town. She did not know much about his daily comings and goings, but of this, she was sure. She decided not to ask.

Grabbing a small plastic bag and the old, tattered book, Kuda hopped out before the car had come to a complete stop. Had he looked back, he may have noticed Maiguru's mild annoyance. He did not. Instead, he dashed to the small informal market behind Beanster, as one frantically looking for another. As it were, he found the man he sought right away.

"*Whatagwan* Don Gorgon!" Kuda clamoured in a comical Jamaican accent.

The man sat on the ground with his back to the wall, basking in the sun with a huge straw hat and surgical mask covering his face. His dreadlocks strayed to just above his waist; it was thus he had earned all manner of nicknames referencing Rastafari culture. He pulled his mask down, looked up with a sneer on his face, to see who beckoned to him.

"It's me Dread. You drew a picture for me some months ago!"

The man did not remember Kuda. Business had been slow—but not that slow.

"Yea… *Wha ya need, mi yut?*" Kuda was annoyed, and slightly embarrassed, by the absence of reciprocal enthusiasm. No time to wallow though.

"I need you to draw another one for me faster faster!"

"*Ah ah, mfanani*, you're rushing me already?"

"*Maya*, Dread! I'm leaving town this afternoon, and I was hoping to have it ready before then."

"Let me see it then."

Kuda shook the old book, and a photo fell out, which he dutifully handed over to the artist.

He inspected it as if it were a historical document, narrowing his eyes as he did.

"*Who dis? Your bredda?*"

"Ye…yes. My brother indeed."

"*Bho.* Give me two hours. Bring me ten dollars then."

Ten dollars was a lot of money. Two hours was a long time. Kuda was not in the mood to bargain on both fronts, so he chose the more pressing one. Maiguru was not going to stick around the shops for two hours and, besides, he had to go.

"*Haa* Dread, two hours? Can we hurry it up? I'll be here, pocketful if you can get it done in an hour!"

The artist sneered. He did not like being rushed. Tourists and suburban people always spoke to him like some houseboy, here for their beck and call. He resented that. However, when he looked up to meet the young man's gaze, he saw not contempt or entitlement, but a subtle desperation: as if much hung on this picture.

"*Bho mfanami.* Come back in an hour then. But bring me the ten, and one or two cigarettes."

It was still a pricey deal for Kuda, but an hour on short notice was asking quite the favour from the artist. Besides, with tourism coming to a near standstill as the virus, and worries about it, spread, the informal economy was withering as well. He could make peace with leaving ten dollars. In any case, Dread always guaranteed a good job. They signed their deal with a lethargic fist-bump, and Kuda walked back towards the entrance of the shopping centre.

The newspaper boy recognised him from a short distance away, and greeted Kuda with an enthusiasm foreign to Kuda.

"Aah Big Man! It's always good to see you! You're not working today?"

"What? Oh. No. Haa, that was just for that day *mfana*. How are you?"

"Haa you know these things, senior. One day is one day. Later will be greater."

"Haha. Later will be greater, huh? Indeed." Kuda hardly ever found much to dwell on in clichés, and the boy had uttered it as just that: a cliché merely rolling off the tongue. Kuda was surprised by how much he liked it.

"Anyway *mfanami*. I was hoping to catch you here."

"Ah ah, me? For the why, *mudhara?*"

"Haha, no, don't worry. I'm leaving town for, ah, I don't know how long. I just wanted to leave something in your custody," Kuda said, as he handed the small plastic bag to the newspaper boy.

The boy opened it, not knowing what to expect. Despite their pleasant encounters, he barely knew this man. He met all sorts of strange people every single day; too many to ever be at ease with even apparent benevolence. His skepticism turned to utter elation when he saw what it was: it was the scarf and shoes!

"Ah *mudhara!* Are you sure? Don't you have people? Why me?"

"Haha, younger. Never question gifts like that. All the misfortune that befalls us, do we get answers? Sometimes good little things come our way, because we are good people. Or maybe because the world needs a bit of balance, you know?"

The boy nodded in agreement. He was too rapt in his gift to engage in Kuda's musings.

"By the way, do you know where I can get a cigarette or two?"

"Haha senior, you smoke too? You don't strike me as the ty…"

"Oh, no. Not at all."

"Wait," the boy said, remembering that he had seen Kuda emerge from behind the building, "is Dread doing a job for you?"

"Haha! How did you know?"

"He likes his cigarettes. Before the virus, he would go across the street every lunch time for a pack. But now, because he's not raking in the customers he used to, he has added the cigarette tax to the few he gets. Hah! Can't stop Dread!" They both chuckled, and the boy continued, "but see, me, I'm a hustler. So, what I do now is, at the beginning of the week, I buy a pack. Me I don't smoke. But I wait to see the people coming from him and, when they get closer, I make a seemingly random comment about selling cigarettes. Everybody buys from me now to go pay Dread— we all win! Haha."

Kuda chuckled again. He was impressed with the boy. He asked how much he owed him for the one cigarette, but the boy was not having it. He insisted that he take one for free. He wrapped his new scarf around his neck and, pulling the cigarette from his pocket like someone from a 1950s film, twirled as he handed it to Kuda, uttering in a comically pretentious tone, "this one is on the house!" They both burst into laughter. "So, you are leaving town, eh? Where are you going, big man? Diaspora?"

"Ah, no. With this virus, are they still letting people in? Haha. No, I'm headed to Watsomba."

"Ah ah! Watsomba? When do you get back to the city?"

"Honestly kid; I don't know. I will be back if and whenever the winds of the ancestors guide me back here."

The boy was rattled by the sudden gravity in the words of his usually jovial acquaintance. After a moment, he broke the heavy silence again.

"At least you're not out here hauling *The Herald*, lies and all, up and down the avenues. Nobody reads anymore, big man. Not the papers, anyway!"

Kuda chuckled mutedly, and the boy continued.

"Haha, Watsomba huh? Where is that? Over there in Manicaland? You got a girl over there? Haha. Big city man like you—what's there for you in deep roots Watsomba?"

"Eish younger. It's been a brutal season," Kuda stared into the distance as he spoke. It was the first time he had allowed himself to acknowledge the gravity of…everything. He looked towards where Maiguru had parked to see if she was on her way back. Not yet. He checked his phone, and saw he had a little under forty minutes before picking up his drawing from Dread.

He sat back against the wall, next to the newspaper boy, and began, "I grew up in Watsomba. My mother died a long long time ago. I came to the city around 2007…The hunger years. I moved in with my uncle and aunt…"

Chapter 21

He arrived in Watsomba just after dusk. Gogo was waiting for him. No sooner had she seen him alight, she broke into a celebratory song and dance, to the muted chuckles of the other passengers. There was a time when Kuda would have been embarrassed. Not today though. It was for this that he had come home. He lumbered down the bus steps with the deceptively casual air of a dignitary, only to immediately turn into the little boy that had left the homestead some thirteen years ago as he collapsed into his grandmother's embrace.

Gogo! Hah! Kuda remembered how, when he left for Harare for the first time many moons ago, it had been thought that Gogo was getting frail in her old age. Here she was still, meeting him at the bus! She had outlived both her sons, and her daughter-in-law. Back then, it would have been inconceivable that Gogo would be at Kurauone's funeral. How strange a hand it is that writes the stories of our journeys on earth!

Anticipating Kuda's bags and groceries from Maiguru, she had brought with her two boys from the village to help carry the load. They left the old woman and erstwhile grandchild to their moment a while longer, picked up the luggage from the side of the bus, and began walking towards the homestead.

Kuda smiled wryly at them and nodded his head in grateful acknowledgement. They reminded him of two little boys he had known once upon a time in Watsomba.

Kuda slept through the night. Frogs and crickets serenaded him to sleep to the oldest tune he had ever known, before aged rooster heralded his presence in Watsomba at dawn.

When the sun was safely within its place atop the skies, Kuda grabbed his tattered book and, separating them from Gogo's groceries, gathered the baby things he had asked Maiguru to buy as well. He strolled along the familiar path that led to Kurauone's homestead. They may have charted it themselves, he and Kurauone. He did not remember now, except that it had always been there.

Mai Loveness spotted him as he emerged from the bushy path. She was bathing her daughter in the front yard of the homestead. He almost expected to hear Kurauone yell out "*Wangu!*" as he had done a thousand times. What Mai Loveness lacked in familiar salutation, she made up for in enthusiasm. She jumped up as she dried her hands and ran towards him to receive him as if he had brought a truckful of goods.

He may as well have. After Kurauone's funeral, and as days turned into seasons, the goodwill had slowly dried up. Perhaps not the goodwill. Despite being a virtual newcomer into her husband's community when he died, she had been fully embraced by the community to this day. The community, as a whole, was struggling and, in this as in many around the world, widows and orphans often bear the brunt of poverty—even among the most benevolent of peoples. The sight of her sobbing at the small parcel he had brought her unsettled Kuda. She must have seen it, as she got up awkwardly from where they now sat and awkwardly began dressing her child. As soon as she was done slapping Vaseline on the fidgety girl's face, Mai Loveness pointed to Kuda and said "Look who's here! Your uncle is here! Daddy's friend is here!"

Perhaps it was her mother's enthused tone. Or perhaps it was the familiar warmth of such words as 'daddy' and 'friend.' Whatever it was, the infant child charged at Kuda as if her very own father was back from the mines. If Kuda had been stoic until then, he held on no longer. He wept as he held the child, for reasons he did not understand. Loveness bore her mother's round face, but the mischievous smirk across her face was unmistakably Kurauone.

He composed himself quickly once he saw that baffled sadness had now usurped Loveness's initial playfulness, and her mother's own tears had only multiplied. He was ashamed. This homestead had been drowned in tears over the past year, what right had he to reflood this drying plain?

Wiping away the last rogue tear, and with Loveness now sitting on his lap, Kuda spoke in elaborate glee.

"I got you something else, child of ours!" she giggled, as he pulled out the tattered book and dug through its pages.

He pulled out the drawing, now laminated and framed (Dread's ten dollars and cigarettes had not been for nought), of Kuda and Kurauone. It was the only picture they had ever taken together, at Gogo's request, on their way to the bus before Kuda left for Harare for the first time.

Mai Loveness came and stood behind them to see what it was as well. She exclaimed amidst laughter, "Wow! That's you two!? Ah! You never changed haha! At least you have the beard now; my poor husband! All the way to the grave looking like a twelve-year-old!" They both laughed, wiping away earlier tears.

"Lavhu! Lavhu! Mai Loveness teased her daughter, "who is that in the picture? Who is that!? Say Da-da!"

"Da-da!" Child replied, clumsily smearing her finger all over that picture. Much needed levity fell over the homestead.

"Ah look at me! My husband dies and I forget all my manners! Should I make you some tea, Uncle Kuda?"

"Haha no *mainini*. Don't worry yourself. I was just about to walk over to see where my brother sleeps before I go back to my old lady."

"Aah really it's no bother! Do you remember where it is, or do you need me to walk you there?"

"Ah ah *mainini!* You arrived here yesterday; I was born into these bushes! I should be showing you around, not vice versa haha! Besides, I just need a moment with him by myself."

She smiled and nodded, "Aah that is well, Uncle Kuda. Stop by here before you walk back home. I was making tea anyway. It will be ready by then."

Glossary

Aizve - Utility expression used to communicate bemusement, dismay, or surprise, akin to "oh!"

Baba - Father of… (standard title by which fathers are addressed.)

Bho - Good

Bhuku ramangwanda - The book of miscellaneous things

Chinja masheets - Change your sheets

Eish - pained expression, akin to "damn!"

Gogo- Grandmother

Hezvo - (see 'aizve.')

Ipapo manje - That part now

Madiiko - What's up?

Mai - Mother of… (standard title by which mothers are addressed.)

Maiguru - aunt; specifically, mother's older sister or father's older brother's wife (the latter in this case.)

Mainini - Aunt: either your mother's younger sister, your father's younger brother's wife or, in this case, used to reference your younger brother's wife. (Complement to Maiguru.)

Mauyu - Baobab fruit

Mazhanje - Wild loquats

Mbuya Nehanda - A maternal spirit among the Shona people, most synonymous with her medium, Charwe, who was one of the early leaders of the anticolonial movement at the tail end of the 19th century.

Mfana/Mfanami - Little brother/kid

Mhai/Mhamha - Mother

Mhomz - Mother (informal)

Mudhara - Literally "old man," but generally a masculine term of jovial reverence, akin to "big man" or 'chief" in other contexts.

Mumwe wangu - My friend! (Literally, 'my other!')

Mwanangu - My Child

Pafeya chaipo - For Real

Saga Bag - Large plastic, typically checkered bag, also known as a 'Ghana-Must-Go Bag' or 'Chinatown Tote Bag', depending on location.

Salisbury - Harare's colonial name

Tibvire mhani apa - a chiding akin to 'stop the nonsense!' or 'get off it!'

Toonana - See you.

Tsono neshinda - Like a needle and thread (an expression of closeness.)

Tsuro Magen'a - Brer rabbit

Wangu - (See "Mumwe Wangu")

Wasu - Nickname for the Manyika people from Zimbabwe's eastern province. Depending on context, it can be a term of endearment, light-heart ribbing, or ridicule.

Wena - You

Zhet - an informal deal for, typically, an informal

money-making endeavour. Generically, also used to mean a thing, enterprise, or system.

About the author

Shingi Mavima is a poet, and writer hailing from
Zimbabwe and currently residing in Toledo Ohio.

Mavima has published two poetry collections,
Homeward Bound and *Mirage of Days Old*, as well
as one autobiographical novel, *Pashena*.

When he is not writing creatively, Mavima is an
Assistant Professor of History at the University of
Toledo. He specialises in contemporary Southern
African history with a focus on the colonial and
postcolonial periods, with additional scholarly
interests in African literature and popular culture.

Printed in the USA
CPSIA information can be obtained
at www.ICGtesting.com
LVHW030717310124
770460LV00070B/1676

9 781914 287619